Lucretia the Unbearable

Lucretia the Unbearable

by Marjorie Weinman Sharmat
illustrated by Janet Stevens

Holiday House, New York

This book is dedicated with great malevolence to
warts, mosquito bites, hangnails, errant sneezes,
and all the other rotten things that inspired it.

Text copyright © 1981 by Marjorie Weinman Sharmat
Illustrations copyright © 1981 by Janet Stevens
All rights reserved
Printed in the United States of America

Library of Congress Cataloging in Publication Data

Sharmat, Marjorie Weinman.
Lucretia the unbearable.

Summary: Because Lucretia Bear is overly concerned
about her health, the other animals don't enjoy being
with her.
[1. Hypochondria—Fiction. 2. Animals—Fiction]
I. Stevens, Janet. II. Title.
PZ7.S5299Lu   [E]   81-1923
ISBN 0-8234-0395-5   AACR2

Lucretia Bear was getting ready for her morning bicycle ride.

She packed lemon drops.
"Because I might get a sore throat."

She packed a handkerchief.
"Because my nose might drip."

She packed a thermometer.
"Because I might get a fever."

She packed bandages.
"Because I might get hurt."

Lucretia got on her bicycle and rode off.

"Good morning," she said to Hunkly Lion.

"You have a wart on your nose," said Hunkly.

Lucretia stopped her bicycle.

"What?" she said.

"A wart on your nose," said Hunkly. "It's a sort of bump, you know."

"I know what a wart is," said Lucretia. "Oh dear. What does mine look like?"

"Like a shriveled, over-salted peanut," said Hunkly.

"Oh!" cried Lucretia. "I feel sick!"

"Come into my house," said Hunkly, "and I'll give you some warm milk."

Lucretia and Hunkly went into Hunkly's house.

Suddenly Lucretia stopped. "What is this I sniff?" she asked.

"Paint," said Hunkly. "I am painting a chair."

"Paint?" said Lucretia. "Paint makes me sick."

"You already are sick," said Hunkly. "Remember?"

"Why are you asking me if I remember?" asked Lucretia. "Do you think I'm losing my memory? Let's see. The wart, the paint, my memory. I am keeping track of everything that's wrong with me."

"Maybe you should go to the doctor," said Hunkly.

"The doctor?" said Lucretia. "His office is full of germs."

"Don't think about that," said Hunkly. "I'll ride over to the doctor with you."

"You're a pal," said Lucretia.

Lucretia and Hunkly got on their bicycles and rode to the doctor's.

Loretta Sue Turtle and Fatso Tiger were sitting in the waiting room.

Lucretia went over to Fatso.
"Do you have any germs?" she inquired.

"Not that I know of," said Fatso.
"Good," said Lucretia,
and she sat down next to Fatso.

Fatso cleared his throat. "Ahem!"

"What was the meaning of that?" asked Lucretia, jumping up. "You just ahemmed. Do you have a sore throat?"

Lucretia didn't wait for Fatso to answer. She went over to Loretta Sue, who was sitting on a couch. "What's wrong with *you*?" Lucretia asked.

"Nothing," said Loretta Sue.

"Then why are you at the doctor's?" asked Lucretia.

"I'm here for my six-month checkup," said Loretta Sue. "The doctor checks my shell for cracks, dents, wear and tear."

"You sound perfect to sit beside," said Lucretia. "I can catch a sore throat but I can't catch a cracked shell."

Lucretia sat down and waited. At last it was her turn to see the doctor. Lucretia went into his office. The doctor shook her hand and coughed in her face.

"You have a cough!" cried Lucretia.

"I know that," said the doctor. "I'm a doctor. I know these things."

"But I'll catch your cough," said Lucretia.

"Well, I certainly hope not," said the doctor. "Now, please tell me why you're here."

"Well, as you can see, I have this wart on my nose," said Lucretia. "I'm also suffering from paint sickness and I'm losing my memory. And now I have a future cough."

"I'd better examine you from head to toe," said the doctor.

"Oh, good," said Lucretia, "because now that you mention *toe,* I think I have a hangnail on my big left toe that's beginning to fester."

The doctor examined Lucretia. Finally, he said, "I don't see anything wrong. In particular, your nose and large left toe are in fantastic shape."

"Well, then, how about my memory?" asked Lucretia. "You can't see my memory."

"Your memory seems fine to me," said the doctor. "You remembered all the problems you don't have."

The doctor coughed again.

Lucretia left quickly. She and Hunkly rode off on their bicycles.

"I don't have anything wrong with me," said Lucretia.

"How terrific," said Hunkly.

Suddenly Lucretia's bicycle hit a rock. "Oooooooo!" she gasped, as the bicycle tipped over. Lucretia fell to the ground. "Help!" she cried. "I'm dead!"

Hunkly got off his bicycle and went to help Lucretia.

"I'm definitely dead," said Lucretia.

"You're not dead," said Hunkly. "All you have is a scraped knee."

"I need a doctor, a nurse, an ambulance, and the fire department,"
said Lucretia.

"Don't be silly," said Hunkly. "All you need is a Band-Aid."

"A lot you know," said Lucretia. "Wait till my blood gushes and squirts and turns the ground all gucky red."

"You're silly and unbearable!" said Hunkly. "I'm going home."
Hunkly got on his bicycle and rode off.

Lucretia limped around, looking for the bandages she had packed. She limped into Loretta Sue Turtle and Fatso Tiger. "Help!" said Lucretia. "I fell off my bicycle, and I'm dead."

Fatso looked at Lucretia. "So now you're dead," he said. "Well, that will keep you from getting a sore throat."

"You have a scraped knee," said Loretta Sue. "I get them all the time. Go home, wash it, put on a Band-Aid, and keep your mouth closed for a week."

Loretta Sue and Fatso walked off.

"Hmpfff!" said Lucretia. She got on her bicycle and started to ride.

"Just wait till *they're* dead. I won't help them one bit!"

Lucretia rode along. "Well, my knee feels a little sore, but I'm riding quite well. So I guess all I have is a little scrape." Then she thought, "A little scrape and a lot of enemies. Hunkly and Fatso and Loretta Sue can't stand me anymore. Maybe I *am* unbearable."

Lucretia started riding around in circles. She thought about all the things that *weren't* wrong with her. "I don't have chicken pox, indigestion, bunions, hay fever, or lots of other things. Do you suppose I'm practically overflowing with good health?" she asked herself.

Lucretia rode home. She bandaged her scraped knee. "That takes care of my knee," she said, "but what can I do about being *unbearable?* I can't put a bandage on *that!*"

Lucretia packed some food in a basket and rode to Hunkly's house.
Hunkly and Fatso and Loretta Sue were sitting outside.

Lucretia took the basket from her bicycle.
"I see you brought your first-aid kit,"
said Hunkly.
"No," said Lucretia. "I only have
a scraped knee. I feel so good.
I want to have a picnic."

Lucretia took some food from her basket, sat down, and started to eat.

"You're not on the lookout for germy flies and ants?" asked Hunkly.

"Or food poisoning?" asked Loretta Sue.

"Or a jaw ache?" asked Fatso.

"No," said Lucretia. "And I'm not even dead anymore. That's how good I feel."

"Very, very glad to hear that," said Hunkly.

"Yes, indeed," said Loretta Sue and Fatso.

They all sat down and joined Lucretia. And nobody ever called her unbearable again.